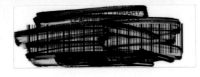

D0569399

APR 0 8

MIRABEAU B. LAMAR

SECOND PRESIDENT OF TEXAS

MIRABEAU B. LAMAR

SECOND PRESIDENT OF TEXAS

Judy Alter

Illustrated by Patrick Messersmith

State House Press

McMurry University

Abilene, Texas

Library of Congress Cataloging-in-Publication Data

Alter, Judy, 1938-
    Mirabeau B. Lamar : second president of Texas / Judy Alter; illustrated by
Patrick Messersmith.
        p. cm.–(Stars of Texas series)
    Includes bibliographical references and index.
    ISBN-13: 978-1-880510-97-1 (hardcover : alk. paper)
    ISBN-10: 1-880510-97-9 (hardcover : alk. paper)
    1. Lamar, Mirabeau Buonaparte, 1798-1859–Juvenile literature. 2. Presidents–
Texas–Biography–Juvenile literature. 3. Texas–Politics and government–To 1846–
Juvenile literature. 4. Texas–History–Republic, 1836-1846–Juvenile literature.
I. Messersmith, Patrick, ill. II. Title. III. Series.

F390.L2A55 2005
976.4'02--dc22

                                                                2005013026

State House Press
McMurry Station, Box 637
Abilene, TX 79697-0637
(325) 793-4682

Distributed by the Texas A&M University Press Consortium
(800) 826-8911 • www.tamu.edu/upress

Printed in the United States of America

ISBN 1-880510-97-9

Book designed by Rosenbohm Graphic Design

The Stars of Texas Series

Other books in this series include:

Henrietta King: Rancher and Philanthropist

CONTENTS

Chapter 1   Introduction 9

Chapter 2   Early Life in Georgia 15

Chapter 3   A Texas Hero 25

Chapter 4   Lamar Enters Public Service 33

Chapter 5   Lamar as President 43

Chapter 6   Private Citizen and Soldier 55

Excerpts from Two Poems 62

Timeline 63

Glossary 65

Further Reading 67

Websites 68

Index 69

Chapter 1

INTRODUCTION

✳✳✳✳✳

Sam Houston dominates the early history of Texas. He was commander-in-chief of the Texas army during the war for independence from Mexico. He served as the first president of the Republic of Texas and then later served a second term as the third president. He was a United States senator and then governor after Texas became a state.

Sam Houston was a large and colorful figure, who attracted attention wherever he went. Sometimes his dress was unusual—moccasins and buckskin. Sometimes his voice was loud, and he was known to curse.

Mirabeau Buonaparte Lamar, the second president of the Republic of Texas, sometimes gets lost in Sam Houston's shadow. But he deserves more attention than he gets. A native of Georgia, Lamar

Mirabeau Buonaparte Lamar was named after the two heroes of the French Revolution— Count Mirabeau and General Napoleon Buonaparte.

was a quiet and mannerly southern gentleman who spoke softly and was always carefully dressed.

Lamar first came to Texas during the war for independence. He showed great courage in rescuing wounded and surrounded Texans during the Battle for San Jacinto. Later he showed the same courage in battle during the Mexican-American War of 1846-1848. Late in his life he served as United States Ambassador to Nicaragua and Costa Rica.

Lamar had many accomplishments during his presidency. He was dedicated to education and wanted to use public lands to finance schools. While he was in office, the Texas legislature passed a bill creating the public school system and two state universities. Because of this, Lamar is known as the Father of Texas Education.

Mirabeau is pronounced MEER-uh-bow. Buonaparte is pronounced BONE-a-part.

Today, several elementary and high schools throughout the state are named Lamar. Lamar State University in Beaumont is named after him. There is also a Lamar County, in northeast Texas on the Arkansas state line. The town of Lamar is located in Aransas County, on the Gulf Coast just north of Corpus Christi. A statue of Lamar stands in the Texas Hall of State in Dallas, and his homes in Richmond and Austin bear historical markers.

Lamar spent long hours writing poetry and is also known as the Poet President of Texas. He was the first president of the Philosophical Society of Texas, which is still in existence today. It exists to encourage research and preserve historical documents about the United States.

Lamar was a charming man with many loyal friends, but he also had some enemies. His strongest enemy was Sam Houston.

During the war for independence, Houston admired Lamar's courage and rapidly promoted him from private to colonel. But the two men were very different, and they disagreed on many things, such as what to do with captured Mexican General Antonio López de Santa Anna, how to treat Texas Indians, statehood for Texas, and other matters. Lamar felt that Houston stood in the way of his political career and his service to Texas.

Mirabeau B. Lamar was a true Texas patriot and a man who made many contributions to the state during its early history. He is important to Texas history, and his accomplishments deserve more recognition today.

Lamar County is located in Northeast Texas. The county seat is Paris.

Chapter 2

EARLY LIFE IN GEORGIA

✳✳✳✳✳

Mirabeau Buonaparte Lamar was born August 16, 1798,

on the Cherry Hill plantation near Louisville, Georgia. He was the

son of John and Rebecca Lamar, and he had three brothers and four

sisters. As Lamar's full name indicates, the family was French.

When Mirabeau was about ten, the family moved to a new

plantation on the Little River, between Eatonton and Milledgeville

in Georgia. The new, two-story house was called Fairfield.

Mirabeau was an active youngster. He liked to help oversee

the farm work and enjoyed horseback riding, fencing, sword fight-

ing, boat trips on the Oconee River and stage trips to Macon,

Georgia.

Mirabeau Lamar had three brothers—Lucius Quintus Cincinnatus, Thomas Randolph, and Jefferson Jackson; he had four sisters—Amelia, Mary Ann, Evalina, and Loretta Rebecca.

But there was a scholarly side to the young man. He went to school in nearby towns, and he loved to read. Sometimes he painted in oils, and he wrote poetry to his girlfriends. He acted in plays and liked to go to dances.

✳✳✳

ON HIS OWN

In 1819 Lamar set off on his own. He and a family friend went to Cahawba, Alabama. Cahawba had just been named the capital of the new state of Alabama, and the two men thought a business would do well there. They opened a general store, but they didn't make any money. Eventually they closed the store. Lamar later admitted that perhaps his nature was too dreamy for the practical work of keeping a store.

Cahawba (later spelled Cahaba) was the capital of Alabama when Lamar moved there. Today the deserted site of the town is a park operated by the Alabama Historical Commission.

Next he tried to put his love of reading and words to use by becoming co-publisher of a newspaper, the *Cahawba Press*. It was one of two weekly newspapers in the new capital. Lamar traveled all over the state, looking for advertisements and trying to understand Alabama politics.

When the Alabama state capital was moved from Cahawba, there was no audience for the newspaper. Lamar and his partner stopped publication, and Lamar went home to Georgia.

George Troup had just been elected governor of Georgia. It was a close and bitter election. Troup won followers by defying United States President John Quincy Adams. Adams had signed a treaty with the Creek Indians in Georgia by which the Creeks gave up most of their land. Troup argued that by an earlier treaty the Creeks had given up all their land. He thought Indian relations were "local matters," not the business of the federal government.

Lamar became Troup's private secretary. His exposure to Troup's Indian policy may well have had an influence on the policy Lamar later would develop in Texas.

While Lamar worked for Governor Troup, the Marquis de Lafayette returned to the United States for a visit. General Lafayette and his country of France had come to the aid of the colonies during the American Revolution. Lamar was the state official who received Lafayette. He was proud of his French heritage and proudly wore a brand new sword for the occasion. He took Lafayette on a tour of the Creek nation. Later he said that visit was the highlight of his time with Governor Troup.

In 1824 Mirabeau won a medal for "excelling in fencing." The medal is on display at the San Jacinto Museum of History near Houston.

Tabitha Jordan was only fourteen years old when Lamar first met her. She was seventeen when they married. He was twenty-eight.

✳✳✳

MARRIAGE

Mirabeau Lamar courted several young women during these years, but it seemed he would always be a bachelor.

He first met Tabitha Jordan in Cahawba when she was only fourteen. He visited the family home several times over the years and finally, in 1824, Lamar asked Tabitha to marry him. She refused. He kept asking. Finally she agreed. They were married January 1, 1826, at her sister's home in Perry County, Alabama.

As the couple returned to Georgia to set up housekeeping, something spooked the horses pulling their carriage. There was a wreck, and Tabitha was thrown onto some rocks. Her face was badly cut. The legend is that her husband took her to an Indian hut and stitched her face with needle and thread. After her face healed, she had only a small scar.

Governor Troup was defeated in the election of 1828, and Lamar was out of a job. He moved his family to Columbus, Georgia, just after the birth of his daughter, Rebecca Ann.

Lamar published the *Columbus Enquirer*. His paper carried mostly political news. Lamar believed in slavery, and he believed in states' rights. He believed that states had the right to withdraw from the union and that many matters like Indian affairs were state matters. The federal government should not interfere.

In his newspaper, he also reviewed books of poetry and acted as a booster for the future of Columbus. In 1829, Lamar ran for office. He was elected state senator from Muscogee County.

✳✳✳

Death of Tabitha Lamar

A second child, son John Burwell, was born while the family was in Columbus. Tabitha was always in frail health, and in 1830 she died of consumption. Mirabeau Lamar was thrown into depression. He left his daughter with his mother and his son with Tabitha's mother and set off to travel and write for two years. His son, John, died before his first birthday.

Mirabeau Lamar's two best-known poems, "At Evening on the Banks of the Chattahoochee" and "Thou Idol of My Soul," were written during his travels. They are elegies to his wife.

In 1832, Lamar returned to Columbus. He decided to run as a candidate for the United States House of Representatives. He was defeated but went on to become active in founding the Georgia States' Rights Party.

He began to publish his newspaper again so he could have a voice for his political views. He studied law and in 1834, he ran for Congress again. He had several opponents and did not win.

About this time, Lamar's father and sister died within weeks of each other. Then his brother, Lucius, a seemingly happy family man and a successful lawyer, committed suicide. Lamar decided once again to travel to ease his grief.

Chapter 3

A Texas Hero

✳✳✳✳✳

James W. Fannin, who would die in the Mexican massacre of Texas troops at Goliad, was a friend of Lamar's. Fannin had written a series of Texas letters describing for the American people the politics and country of Texas. These letters convinced Lamar to go to Texas. Texas was then a Mexican province.

Lamar arrived in Texas in July 1835. He traveled around Texas collecting letters, stories, and official documents. Someday he intended to write a history of Texas, but he never completed it. Today the notes he took are called the Lamar Papers and are in the Texas State Archives in Austin. They are important sources for information about early-day Texas history.

When the Texians attacked the Mexicans at San Jacinto, a fife played "Come to the Bower." It is a love song, not a military marching song.

Texas was in turmoil. The Mexican government had forbidden any more settlers to come from the United States. Texians held conventions to demand certain privileges from the Mexican government. Empresario Stephen F. Austin, leading spokesperson for Texians, was imprisoned in Mexico City. Lamar wanted to live in Texas and be part of the exciting drive for freedom from Mexico. He returned to Georgia to put his affairs in order so he could move to Texas.

General Antonio López de Santa Anna, dictator of Mexico, directed Mexican troops who massacred between 189 and 257 Texians at the Alamo mission in San Antonio. Later Mexican soldiers executed nearly five hundred Texian prisoners at the presidio of La Bahía (now the town of Goliad). Lamar's friend, General James W. Fannin, was in command and was among those killed.

When Lamar heard the news, he hurried back to Texas. He rode his horse to death in his haste to join the Texas army and had to finish the trip on foot.

✳✳✳

BRAVERY ON THE BATTLEFIELD

Lamar found the army at Groce's Point, near present-day Hempstead outside Houston. He enlisted in Houston's army as a private.

Morale in the Texas army was not high. Many enlisted men accused Houston of cowardice because he refused to fight, but Houston knew his army had only one battle in it and he wanted to choose the right place. Finally he isolated Santa Anna's major force at San Jacinto. He had one of his men, Deaf Smith—for whom a Texas county is now named—destroy the one

After the Battle of San Jacinto, Mirabeau Lamar wrote a poem entitled "San Jacinto." Excerpts of the poem are on page 62.

bridge that would have made retreat possible for either army. Still, Houston refused to attack. His soldiers grew angrier.

The two armies exchanged gunfire several times before the actual battle. Lamar, who was not a warlike man, showed great bravery.

The Texians had two cannons, but a group of about sixty men decided to steal a Mexican cannon, without telling Houston. The Mexicans turned them back, but the horse ridden by nineteen-year-old Walter Paye Lane got excited and rode straight for the Mexican side instead of retreating with the other Texas fighters. Lane fought with a Mexican officer, but his gun was empty and he missed with his pistol. Finally he knocked the man senseless with the pistol, but another Mexican rode up and ran a spear through

Lamar enlisted as a private a few days before San Jacinto. A few days after San Jacinto, he was named secretary of war; not long after that he became commander in chief for a short time.

Lane's shoulder. The young man fell off his horse, landed on his head, and passed out.

The Mexican officer was about to kill Lane, when Lamar shot the officer. Lamar thought Lane was dead, but the young man lived and praised Lamar for saving his life.

Later, Mexicans surrounded Texas Secretary of War Thomas Rusk. Lamar rushed the crowd of Mexican soldiers and created a gap through which Rusk could escape. The Mexicans were so impressed with Lamar's courage that they cheered.

General Houston heard of Lamar's bravery and promoted him to full colonel, which means he jumped quite a few ranks between private and colonel.

The fate of Texas was decided at the Battle of San Jacinto. Houston deliberately began the attack in mid-afternoon, catching the Mexicans, including Santa Anna, at their siesta.

Lamar led sixty cavalry soldiers into the battle. A total of about nine hundred men attacked the Mexicans. In a twenty-minute battle, 630 Mexican soldiers died, 208 were wounded, and 730 were taken prisoner. The Texas army lost only nine men, with thirty wounded. One of the wounded was General Houston, who suffered an ankle wound. His favorite horse, Saracen, was killed under him.

After the battle, Texians discovered that Santa Anna had disguised himself as a poor soldier in the ranks. He was brought to Sam Houston, amid cries from Houston's army for his immediate execution.

Houston and Texas President David G. Burnet thought Santa Anna was more valuable alive than dead. Lamar disagreed with this decision. He felt that the man who had led the Mexicans at the Alamo and given the order to kill Texians at Goliad should be put to death.

Chapter 4

LAMAR ENTERS PUBLIC SERVICE

※※※※※

After the battle, Sam Houston sailed for New Orleans

for treatment of his severe ankle wound. President Burnet planned

to replace the controversial Houston as commander in chief with

Thomas Rusk and asked Mirabeau Lamar to accept appointment to

Rusk's position as secretary of war. Lamar agreed.

The Texas government signed two treaties with Santa Anna,

still being held prisoner. In a public treaty, the Mexican general agreed

to remove all Mexican troops from Texas in an orderly retreat and to

exchange prisoners. In a private treaty, in return for safe passage by

boat to Mexico, Santa Anna agreed to recognize Texas as an indepen-

dent nation, with its southern boundary at the Rio Grande River.

Texas was an independent nation from 1836 to 1845. The leader of Texas was called president until Texas became a state. The head of the state government is now called governor.

Some members of Burnet's cabinet disagreed strongly with these treaties, including secretary of the navy Robert Potter and Lamar. Lamar submitted a statement in opposition. He said Santa Anna could not be trusted and he would not be useful to Texas. He also insisted that Santa Anna should be tried for murder and executed.

As leader of the army, Thomas Rusk was also increasingly critical of government policy and did not discipline the rebellious soldiers who called for Santa Anna's death. Burnet decided to replace Rusk with Lamar as commander in chief, but the soldiers would not accept Lamar. They were loyal to Rusk. Lamar briefly retired to civilian life.

On the first Monday in September 1836, Texians went to the polls to elect their first officers and Congress.

Sam Houston was elected president and Mirabeau B. Lamar vice president.

Mirabeau Lamar was known for always wearing old-fashioned baggy pants.

✳✳✳

VICE PRESIDENT OF THE REPUBLIC OF TEXAS

Almost immediately Houston and Lamar disagreed. Houston sent Santa Anna to Washington to bargain with President Andrew Jackson for recognition of Texas independence and purchase of Texas from Mexico by the United States. Lamar still condemned the lenient treatment of Santa Anna and did not favor Texas becoming part of the United States. When Santa Anna returned to Mexico, he did not keep his pledge to recognize Texas' independence. Texians were angry at Houston.

The Cherokee Nation provided another area of disagreement. During the war with Mexico, the interim government of Texas recognized Cherokee rights to land in East Texas that had been granted them by Mexico. Houston had lived with the Cherokee in Texas and was sympathetic to them. He pushed for ratification of a treaty confirming the Cherokee right to the land. Tribal law, not Texas law, would prevail within these lands. In return, the Cherokee pledged to be neutral in any forthcoming difficulties between Mexico and Texas. The Texians had hoped that the Cherokee would join them in taking up arms against Mexico.

Houston said it was urgent the treaty go into effect so the Cherokee would not side with Mexico. Lamar advised delay. The Senate committee took months to study the treaty and issue a report that finally advised against ratification. Houston's arguments fell on deaf ears, and he felt it was as much opposition to him as to the policy.

Lamar was one of twenty-six Texians who organized the Philosophical Society of Texas in 1837. He was its first president. The organization is still active today.

As Houston had predicted, Mexican agents began to work with the Indian tribe. The Cherokee started a battle near Nacogdoches in the fall of 1838, and Houston was forced to send General Thomas Rusk into the area to quiet things. Relations with the Cherokee quickly deteriorated into a series of small battles.

Houston did not often consult Lamar, and presiding over the Senate took little of his time, so Lamar was free to work on his papers and his proposed history. The unexpected death of Stephen F. Austin in January 1837 prompted Lamar to think of writing the empresario's biography. He advertised in a newspaper for pertinent materials and began to interview leaders from the colonial period. With a possible biography of Santa Anna in mind, Lamar taught himself Spanish. Nothing came of either project.

Lamar traveled to Georgia for six months to visit his daughter and other friends and relatives. When he returned to Texas, supporters urged him to run for president. By law, Houston could not succeed himself in a second term.

Some members of the Texas Senate drafted an inquiry, urging Lamar to run. Houston was not popular in East Texas because of his pro-Indian attitude. Lamar did not want to oppose Thomas Rusk, if he should plan to run, but Rusk assured him he did not want to be in public office. He wanted to develop his new law practice. Rusk was probably Houston's first choice. Lamar decided to run for president.

✳✳✳

PRESIDENTIAL CAMPAIGN

Houston did not support Lamar. He endorsed Peter Grayson, who had been attorney general and had worked for diplomatic recognition of Texas after the Battle of San Jacinto. Houston often spoke on

The Fort Bend Courthouse lawn in Richmond, Texas, has a statue of Lamar.
It was put up in 1936 to mark one hundred years of independence from Mexico.

Grayson's behalf, knowing that the fact that Grayson had not fought in the war, as Lamar had, would work against him. But by now Houston's policies had lost favor with Texians, although he himself remained personally popular.

During the summer campaign, Peter Grayson shocked everyone by committing suicide in Tennessee. He left a note attributing his death to depression, which he had suffered since he was a young man.

Houston next endorsed James W. Collinsworth, chief justice of the Texas Supreme Court. Houston and his friends overlooked the fact that Collinsworth was not old enough to meet the requirements for the presidency. Unfortunately, Collinsworth was an alcoholic. He ended the campaign suddenly by jumping to his death from a steamer in Galveston Bay in July.

The Houston group nominated a third candidate, Robert Wilson, a businessman who had sat in the Texas Senate. He was almost totally unknown. Lamar defeated him by 6,995 to 252.

Mirabeau B. Lamar had been a resident of Texas for only three years and had gone from the rank of private in the army to president of the Republic.

David G. Burnet, former interim president of the Republic, was elected Lamar's vice president, in spite of accusations about his easy treatment of Santa Anna. He ran on Lamar's ticket.

Chapter 5

LAMAR AS PRESIDENT

✳✳✳✳✳

The inauguration of Mirabeau Lamar and David Burnet was scheduled for December 1, 1838, in Houston. As outgoing chief executive, Sam Houston was called on to make a few brief remarks. He spoke for over three hours, describing in detail the accomplishments of his administration.

Lamar was angry. He handed his prepared speech to his personal secretary to read and left the ceremony. The secretary read it in a monotone, and no one was impressed.

Lamar gave his inaugural speech to the Texas Congress a few days later. He described the policies that would guide his administration.

Mirabeau Lamar is known as the "Poet-President" of the Republic of Texas and the Father of Texas Education.

The "Indian problem" was high on his list of concerns. He insisted that the Cherokee had never received good title to their land from Mexico or the Republic of Texas. Treaties giving them land had never been ratified. They were entitled to no money from the government, and any disturbance on their part would be dealt with severely. Lamar recommended increased funds for frontier defense.

Texas had no money. Lamar intended to seek a loan from the United States and to create a national bank, with a portion of public lands used as security. He said he would continue to fight Mexico if peace was not possible. He was not in favor of becoming a part of the United States, especially because the American government did not seem particularly interested. Lamar recommended establishing trade and diplomatic relations with other countries.

President Lamar said, "A cultivated mind is the guardian genius of democracy." That later became the motto of the University of Texas.

✳✳✳

THE INDIAN CRISIS

One of the first major crises in Lamar's presidency involved the Cherokee Indians. A plot was uncovered that linked the Cherokee directly to Mexico City, proving that the Cherokee uprisings in East Texas were started by the Mexican government.

Lamar ordered the army to occupy the Cherokee land and pay the Indians only for improvements on the land, not the land itself. Talks with Cherokee chiefs got nowhere, and fighting followed. Many Cherokee were killed, including Sam Houston's good friend, Chief Bowles.

The Indians retreated to Arkansas, which was what Lamar wanted all along. He had made East Texas safe for settlement and stopped the Mexican government.

The "Indian problem" was far from solved. To the West, the Comanche robbed, kidnapped, and killed settlers regularly. A meeting was called in San Antonio, and the Comanche leaders were guaranteed safety if they would bring in all their prisoners and return stolen property. They arrived with one prisoner—a young girl named Matilda Lockhart. She had been badly abused, including having her nose burned off by repeated thrusts of fiery sticks.

The Indian leaders were invited inside the Council House to negotiate. Once inside, they realized they were hostages and called for help from members of the tribe who waited in the courtyard outside. The Council House battle followed.

Indians terrified San Antonio residents by appearing at their homes and on the streets, chased by army members. Thirty-five Indians were killed and many more wounded; seven Texians died and eight were seriously wounded.

Almost forty schools are named for President Lamar. The first school was Lamar Elementary School in El Paso, opened in 1906. Lamar University in Beaumont is also named for him.

The Comanche wanted revenge. Several months later five hundred braves attacked the settlements of Victoria and Linnville. A few citizens were killed in Victoria, but in Linnville at least twenty-three settlers died and all buildings but one were destroyed. The town was never rebuilt, and most citizens moved to LaVaca.

The Indians stole supplies, horses, and mules and rode away victorious, but Texas troops caught up with them at Plum Creek. The Comanche were defeated in that battle and never again had the force to attack major settlements, though they continued to threaten small settlements through the Civil War.

✳✳✳

The Santa Fe Expedition

Lamar inherited a government with no money and a huge debt. He hoped for a loan from the United States, but the U.S. had just survived the national financial panic of 1837. The loan proved to be a little less than one-tenth the $5 million Lamar had hoped for. Representatives were sent abroad to apply for loans, but they were unsuccessful. Texas was more deeply in debt than ever. Its paper money had little value.

Lamar decided that one way to raise money would be to annex the Spanish settlements around Santa Fe and Taos, in present-day New Mexico. Santa Fe was a trading center that could add money to the Texas treasury. Always a dreamer, Lamar envisioned a trade route from Santa Fe to Cuba, all bringing money to Texas.

The Daughters of the Republic of Texas celebrate Texas Honor Days to honor various Texas heroes. They chose January 26th as Lamar Day. Lamar signed the law creating Texas public schools on January 26, 1839.

Sam Houston loudly opposed this plan, saying the financial benefits were unlikely and it would jeopardize the shaky peace with Mexico. But Lamar convinced Congress, and an expedition marched toward Santa Fe in June 1841.

Two hundred and seventy soldiers and volunteers left Austin, accompanied by merchants and journalists. Twenty-one wagons carried $200,000 worth of trade goods and supplies such as sugar, coffee, and beef, but no vegetables or flour. Later the men suffered terribly from thirst and the lack of bread.

Maps were not good in those days, and the expedition did not realize how far it was to Santa Fe. The march was expected to be about 450 miles; it turned out to be about a thousand miles. Nearing Santa Fe, Mexican troops captured the entire Texas force without firing a shot. The prisoners were marched overland to Mexico City and imprisoned.

It was the low point of Lamar's presidency, and it emphasized the biggest failure of his administration. He had not achieved lasting peace with Mexico.

✳✳✳

DISAGREEMENTS WITH SAM HOUSTON

With Mexico threatening to attack again, Lamar sent the Second Texas Navy to sea (the first had protected the coast during the war for independence). This provided another area of disagreement with Houston, who thought a navy was unnecessary and called the sailors a bunch of pirates. When Houston was elected again, he disbanded the navy and left the ships to rot in Galveston.

Houston and Lamar also disagreed about statehood. Houston believed it would be to Texas' best advantage to become a state within the United States. The U.S. would then protect Texas from Mexico, financing would be eased, and other advantages would follow. Lamar, ever the dreamer, thought Texas should remain independent and one day expand to the Pacific Ocean.

✳✳✳

Major Achievements as President

One of Lamar's major achievements was moving the state capital to Austin.

During the time leading up to war and the war itself, the capital moved several times so the government could avoid capture. After the war, Houston settled the government in a hastily built city bearing his name. It was less a city than a collection of shacks and unpaved roads.

As president, Mirabeau Lamar approved the design of the Lone Star flag that Texas still uses today.

Even while campaigning, Lamar said he would prefer a capital more in the center of the Republic. The story is that Lamar and several friends camped on a hill overlooking the Colorado River, and he decided that was the place for the state capital. Today that hill is Capitol Hill. Temporary buildings were put up— a capitol building, living quarters and an office for the president, and a treasury building.

Another accomplishment of Lamar's was gaining some international recognition for Texas. When he became president, only the United States recognized the Republic. During his term, recognition came from Belgium, the Netherlands, France, and Great Britain.

But the establishment of the educational system remains Lamar's greatest achievement.

At his urging Congress passed a law in 1839 putting aside land in each county for a school, plus land in the state for two universities. The next year Congress gave counties land that could be sold if the proceeds went to public education. These laws laid the groundwork for the public school system, but during the entire period of the Republic only one system—Houston—was established. Congress issued charters to nineteen colleges, nine of which were actually opened.

Lamar could not succeed himself as president, and in 1841 Sam Houston was again elected. Lamar retired to his home in Richmond (in the Houston area).

His presidency might be summed up as one of great vision for Texas that reached beyond what was possible or practical. He established the foundation of a school system, but he left the Republic more heavily in debt than ever. And his record was spoiled by the failure of the Santa Fe Expedition.

Chapter 6

PRIVATE CITIZEN AND SOLDIER

✱✱✱✱✱

In 1843 Mirabeau Lamar traveled to Georgia with his daughter, Rebecca Ann, who had been living with him in Texas. She returned to Georgia because of better educational opportunities.

That summer she died of yellow fever, a disease like malaria that is carried by mosquitoes. Lamar wrote an elegy for her, "On the Death of My Daughter," and once again traveled to relieve his grief.

When he returned to Texas, he became convinced that statehood was best in order to protect slavery in Texas and to prevent the Republic from being a satellite of Great Britain. Texas officially became a state in 1845. The Mexican War began on April 15, 1846, partly over Texas, which Mexico still claimed.

Mirabeau Lamar wrote many poems in his lifetime, beginning as a boy.

✳✳✳

THE MEXICAN WAR

When war broke out, Mirabeau B. Lamar raised a company of volunteers and joined the United States Army under General Zachary Taylor. He was named Inspector General and was made a captain of the Texas Mounted Volunteers on the Rio Grande.

Once again he distinguished himself in battle. In one instance he refused to let a soldier charge up a hill to see if Mexicans were waiting to ambush the United States soldiers. Lamar went in the soldier's place.

He would have preferred to see action in the interior of Mexico, and he blamed his old enemy, Sam Houston, for keeping him sidelined in Laredo. By now, the bitterness between them was so open that Houston referred to Lamar as "Miraboo." Lamar called Houston "The Big Drunk," a nickname others also used for Houston. Lamar called Texas "the Big Drunk's ranch."

Later, Lamar organized a municipal government in Laredo and represented Nueces and San Patricio counties in the Texas legislature.

After the war, Lamar continued to be active in politics for a while. There was some talk of his running for the United States Senate, but the position eventually went to Houston. Lamar did run for Speaker of the Texas House but was defeated. He was named chair of the committee on state affairs but took little interest in the work. In 1849 he retired to Richmond again, intending to write his history of Texas.

In 1851 in New Orleans, he met and married Henrietta Maffitt of Galveston. She was twenty-four; Lamar was fifty-three. Although she was engaged to someone else at the time, Lamar courted her by writing

A collection of more than eighty of Lamar's poems was published in 1938, seventy-eight years after he died. It was called "The Life and Poems of Mirabeau B. Lamar." Only one thousand copies were printed, so it is a rare book today.

To.

Miss Henrietta Maffitt.

O, lady, if the stars so bright,
　　Were diamond worlds bequeath'd to me,
I would resign them all this night,
　　To frame one welcome lay to thee;
For thou art dearer to my heart,
　　Than all the gems of earth and sky;
And he who sings thee as thou art
　　May boast a song that cannot die.

But how shall I the task essay?—
　　Can I rejoin the tuneful throng,
Since Beauty has withdrawn its ray—
　　The only light that kindles song?
No, no—my harp in darkness bound,
　　Can never more my soul beguile;
Its spirit fled when woman frown'd,
　　Nor hopes for her returning smile.

Then blame me not—my skill is gone—
　　I have no worthy song to give;
But thou shalt be my favorite one,
　　To love and worship whilst I live;
What e'er betides—where'er I roam,
　　Thine Angel image I will bear
Upon my heart, as on a stone,
　　In deathless beauty sculptur'd there.

love poems to her. They traveled to Georgia on their honeymoon. Their daughter, Loretto Evalina, was born in Georgia. Then they returned to country life in Richmond.

✳✳✳

AMBASSADOR TO NICARAGUA

Lamar, never a rich man, was in debt and needed income. He applied for a diplomatic position, and in 1857 President James Buchanan offered him the post of United States minister to Nicaragua. The salary would help him clear his debt.

Lamar accepted, even though it would mean being away from his family. Before he left for Central America, he published *Verse Memorials*, a book of his poetry.

Lamar found his diplomatic post increasingly difficult. He was unable to negotiate the treaties he had

Mirabeau and Henrietta Lamar were so poor that Henrietta had to sell butter made from their cows' cream.

Lamar County was one of only fourteen counties in Texas that voted not to secede in 1861. The vote was 553 for and 663 against leaving the Union. However, once Texas decided to secede, Lamar County joined the rest of the state as part of the Confederacy.

been sent to put into effect. He was heavily criticized, although President Buchanan supported him. In 1859 he returned to the U.S., reported his findings in Washington, D.C., and hurried home to his wife and daughter in Richmond. He had no further interest in politics or public life.

On December 19, Lamar told the doctor he thought he was dying. Within minutes, he was dead from a heart attack.

A little more than a year after Lamar's death, Texas became part of the Confederacy, as did Alabama and Georgia, the two southern states where he had lived. Lamar would have approved, because he still believed at the end of his life that states should have the right to withdraw from the union.

But even with Lamar gone, his battle with Houston raged on. Houston did not believe states should leave the Union. He was forced out as governor after Texas voted to secede.

Mirabeau Lamar is buried in Richmond, Texas.

EXCERPTS FROM TWO POEMS
by Mirabeau B. Lamar

FROM "SAN JACINTO"

The rushing armies meet,
And while they pour their breath,
The strong earth trembles at their feet,
And day grows dim with death.

Now launch upon the foe
The lightnings of your rage!
Strike the assailing tyrants low,
The monsters of the age!

They yield! They break! They fly!
The victory is won!
Pursue! They faint, they fall, they die!
O stay! the work is done.

FROM "ON THE DEATH OF MY DAUGHTER"

The morning star that fades from sight
Still beams upon the mind;
So doth her beauty leave the light
Of memory behind.

Though lost to earth—too early gone—
By others seen no more
She is to me still shining on,
And brighter than before.

Timeline

1798—born at Cherry Hill plantation, Georgia

1808—family moves to Fairfield plantation, near Milledgeville

1819—moves to Cahawba, Alabama, tries unsuccessfully to operate a store; teaches at Cahawba Academy; publishes *Cahawba Press*; eventually returns to Georgia

1826—marries Tabitha Jordan

1827—daughter, Rebecca Ann Lamar, born

1829—elected state senator for Muscoggee County

1830—son, John Burwell Lamar, born; Tabitha dies of tuberculosis

1830-1832—travels for two years

1831—son, John, dies

1832—returns to Columbus, Georgia; runs unsuccessfully for state senate

1833—sister and father die

1834—brother kills himself

1835—arrives in Nacogdoches, Texas

1836—joins Texas army; elected vice president of the Republic of Texas

1837—visits Georgia for six months

1838—elected president of the Republic of Texas

1839—establishes Texas public school system

1841—General Sam Houston elected to second term as president of the Republic of Texas

1843—Lamar returns to Georgia to visit his daughter; Rebecca dies later the same year

1845—proposes to Cassandra Flint in Macon, Georgia, but she rejects him

1846-1848—serves as inspector/general in Laredo during Mexican-American War

1851—meets and marries Henrietta Maffitt

1852—second daughter, Loretto Evalina, born; family moves to Richmond, Texas

1857—serves as United States minister to Nicaragua and Costa Rica; poetry published in *Verse Memorials*

1859—returns to family in Richmond; dies of a heart attack on December 19 at the age of sixty-one.

GLOSSARY

The Alamo—the Franciscan mission in San Antonio. Texians occupied the mission, but they were overrun by the Mexican army on March 6, 1836; not one Texian survived.

Consumption—a disease of the lungs; today it is known as tuberculosis.

Depression—a condition of greater and longer lasting sadness and gloom than should be caused by events in a person's life

Dictator—a person who assumes total control over a country and its government

Elegy—a sad poem mourning the dead

Empresario—a settler given the right by the Mexican government to establish a colony and invite other settlers to Texas

Goliad—the town where General James W. Fannin's men were executed by the Mexican army at the La Bahia mission; during the war for independence, the word "Goliad" referred to the massacre, not to the town.

Hostage—someone held as security until a certain act is performed or money paid

Interim government—a temporary government; in this case, a government to rule until proper elections could be held after the end of the war

Presidio—a Spanish military post

Ratification—the act of confirming and making legal a document or agreement

Satellite—in this case, a country that is dependent on a larger country and overshadowed by it

Siesta—an afternoon nap, most usually taken in Spanish countries

States rights—the rights belonging to the state, in contrast to those given to the federal government by the United States Constitution

Texian—an Anglo resident of Texas; this term was used until about 1850

FURTHER READING

Peggy Caravantes. *An American in Texas—The Story of Sam Houston*. Greensboro, NC: Morgan Reynolds Publishing, 2003. A biography of Houston as a teacher, military hero, Indian Bureau agent, lawyer, duelist, and statesman.

Jean Fritz. *Make Way for Sam Houston*. New York: Putnam, 1998. A biography of Houston with quotes from him and his acquaintances.

Isabel R. Marvin. *One of Fannin's Men: A Survivor at Goliad*. Houston, TX: Hendrick-Long Publishers, 1997. The story of one of the few survivors of the massacre that killed Mirabeau Lamar's good friend, James Fannin.

Elizabeth Dearing Morgan. *President Mirabeau B. Lamar*. Austin: Eakin Press, 1994. A biography for readers ages 9-12.

Conrad Stein. *The Story of the Lone Star Republic*. Chicago: Childrens Press, 1988. The history of Texas from the first American settlements in the 1820s to statehood in 1845.

Mary Dodson Wade. *The Road to San Jacinto*. Auburndale, MA: Eye-witness accounts from presidents, homemakers, soldiers, and slaves who took part in events that shaped the Republic of Texas.

Websites

http://www.tsha.utexas.edu/handbook/online/aritcles/view/LL/fla15.html—a historical account of Lamar's life

http://www.tsl.state.tx.us/treasures/giants/lamar/lamar-01.html—a biography of Lamar with links to several related sites about the Republic of Texas, its constitution, and similar topics.

http://www.tsl.state.tx.us/mcardle/sanjac/sanjac119.html *(photo of Lamar at San Jacinto)*

www.lsjunction.com/people/lamar.htm—a short biography with a picture

http://wywy.essortment.com/mirabeaublamar_rqpc.htm—an account of the educational and political contributions of Lamar as president and of his place in Texas history.

Index

A
Adams, President John Quincy, 18
Alamo, 26, 31
Austin, city of, 50, 52
Austin, Stephen F., 26, 38

B
Bowles, Chief (Cherokee), 46
Buchanan, President James, 59, 60
Burnet, David G., 31, 34, 41, 43

C
Cahawba, Alabama, 16, 18, 20
Cahawba Press, 18
Capitol Hill, 53
Cherokee Nation, 37, 38, 44, 46
Civil War, 48
Collinsworth, James W., 40
Colorado River, 52
Columbia Enquirer, 21
Comanche Indians, 47, 48
Confederacy, 60
Costa Rica, 10
Council House battle, 47
Creek Indians, 18-19

F
Fairfield, 15
Fannin, James W., 25-28

G

Georgia States Rights Party, 22
Goliad (La Bahía), 25, 26, 31
Grayson, Peter, 39-40
Groce's Point, 28

H

Houston, city of, 52, 54
Houston, Sam, 9, 13, 52
    and the Cherokee Nation, 37, 46
    death, 60
    disagreements with Lamar, 43, 49, 51, 56-57, 60
    during Texas Revolution, 28, 30, 31, 33
    President of Republic of Texas, 36, 39, 54

J

Jackson, President Andrew, 36
Jordan, Tabitha, see Lamar, Tabitha Jordan

L

Lafayette, Marquis de, 19
Lamar, city, 12
Lamar County, 12
Lamar, Evalina Loretto, 59
Lamar, Henrietta Maffitt, 57
Lamar, John, 15
Lamar, John Burwell, 22
Lamar, Mirabeau Buonoparte
    as Poet President, 12, 44, 58
    as soldier, 56-69
    Philosophical Society of Texas, 12, 38
    vice-president of Republic of Texas, 36
    president of the Republic, 43
Lamar Papers (Texas State Archives), 25
Lamar, Rebecca (mother), 15
Lamar, Rebecca Ann, 21, 39, 55

Lamar State University, 12
Lamar, Tabitha Jordan, 20, 22
Lane, Walter Paye, 29-30
LaVaca, Texas, 48
Linnville, Texas, 48
Lockhart, Matilda, 47

M
Maffitt, Henrietta, see Lamar, Henrietta Mafitt
Mexican-American War, 10, 55-59

N
Navy, Second Texas, 51
Nicaragua, 10, 59-60

P
Plum Creek, 48
Potter, Robert, 34

R
Richmond, Texas, 54, 57, 59
Rio Grande River, 33
Rusk, Thomas, 30, 34, 39

S
San Jacinto, Battle of, 10, 30, 39
Santa Anna, Antonio López de, 13, 26, 31, 33, 34, 36, 38, 41
Santa Fe Expedition, 48-50, 54
Saracen (horse), 31
Smith, Deaf, 28
Statehood for Texas, 51, 55

T
Taylor, General Zachary, 56
Troup, George, 18-19, 21

V
Victoria, Texas, 48

W
Wilson, Robert, 41